Rabbit looks sad.
"Oh dear," says Rabbit.
"What is it?" says Dragon.
"What is it?" say the bees.
"There are men in the wood," says Rabbit.
"What do they want?" say the bees.
"They want Dragon," says Rabbit.

DRAGON'S HIDING PLACE

BY
LUCY KINCAID

ILLUSTRATED BY
ERIC KINCAID

Brimax . Newmarket . England

Dragon lives in the wood.
The bees are his friends.
He hums songs with them.
One day, Rabbit comes to
see them.

Dragon goes with Rabbit.
The bees go with Rabbit.
They see the men.
They hide behind a tree.
They watch. They listen.
The men have a net.
"We will catch the
dragon," say the men. "We
will put the dragon in a
cage."

Dragon is afraid.

"What can I do?" says Dragon.

"You must hide," says Rabbit.

It is too late. The men see Dragon. They run after him.

Rabbit gets under their feet. He trips them up.

The bees buzz round the men.

Dragon gets away.

Dragon looks for a place to hide. He sees a hole in a tree.
Dragon gets into the hole.
"What are you doing in the tree?" says Badger.
"I am hiding," says Dragon.
"I can see you," says Badger.
"What can I do?" says Dragon.

"Men are coming. They want to put me in a cage," says Dragon.

"I will help you," says Badger.

Badger rolls logs in front of the hole.

Nobody can see the hole.

Nobody can see Dragon.

Badger goes on his way.

The men come. They have
a net. They have sticks.
"Where is that dragon?"
say the men.
Dragon keeps very still.
The men do not see him.
The men go away.

It is safe. Dragon can come out.
Where is Dragon hiding?
Nobody knows.
The animals look for Dragon.
Nobody can find him.

Dragon is still inside the tree. He knows it is safe to come out.
He cannot get out.
He cannot move the logs.
"I will shout," says Dragon. "The animals will hear me."

Dragon opens his mouth.
But he knows he must not
shout.
He is a dragon. Dragons
spit fire when they shout.
Fire will burn the tree.
''I know what to do,'' says
Dragon.

Dragon begins to hum.
He hums as loud as he
can.
"Hum Hum HUM HUM."
Dragon's friends hear the
humming.
"Only Dragon can hum like
that," say the bees. "He
must be inside the tree."

They try to move the logs.
They cannot.
Badger comes to the tree.
Badger wants to help
Dragon.
"There is nobody in that
tree," says Badger.
"Yes, there is," says
Rabbit. "Dragon is in the
tree. We can hear him
humming."

"Dragon is our friend," say the bees. "It is safe for him to come out now."
"Then I will help you," says Badger.
They roll the logs away from the hole.
Dragon gets out.
"I am glad to see you all," says Dragon.
"And we are glad to see you," say his friends.

Say these words again

watch	sticks
loud	nobody
catch	shout
cage	fire
their	Badger
buzz	afraid
only	knows